The Fly Flew In

The Fly Flew In

by David Catrow

I Like to Read®

SCHOLASTIC INC.

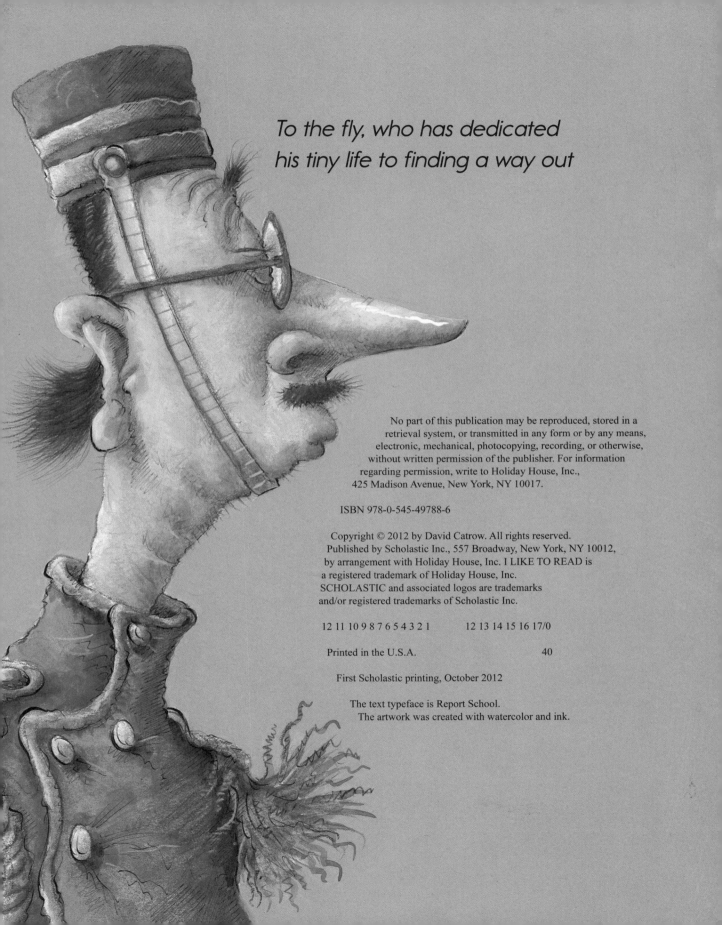

*To the fly, who has dedicated
his tiny life to finding a way out*

ISBN 978-0-545-49788-6

Copyright © 2012 by David Catrow. All rights reserved.
Published by Scholastic Inc., 557 Broadway, New York, NY 10012,
by arrangement with Holiday House, Inc. I LIKE TO READ is
a registered trademark of Holiday House, Inc.
SCHOLASTIC and associated logos are trademarks
and/or registered trademarks of Scholastic Inc.

12 11 10 9 8 7 6 5 4 3 2 1   12 13 14 15 16 17/0

Printed in the U.S.A.   40

First Scholastic printing, October 2012

The text typeface is Report School.
The artwork was created with watercolor and ink.

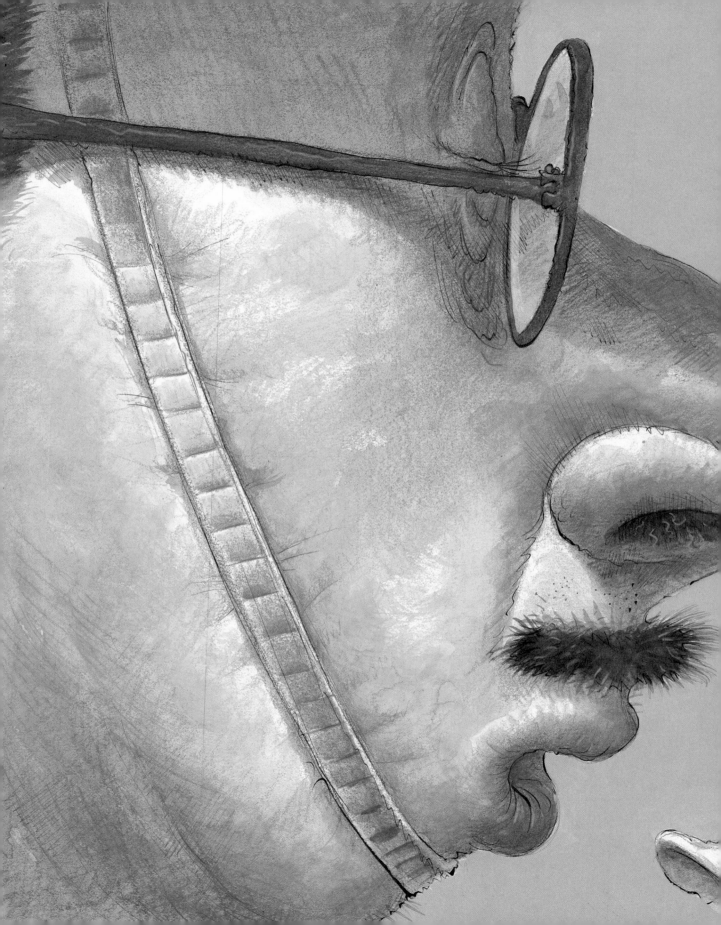

The fly flew on.

The fly flew off.

The fly got in line.
Flick!

The fly did a flip.

The fly flew in,
out, and on.

He landed on a lollipop.
Yuck!

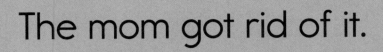

The mom got rid of it.

The fly flew by.

Get that fly!
Boom!

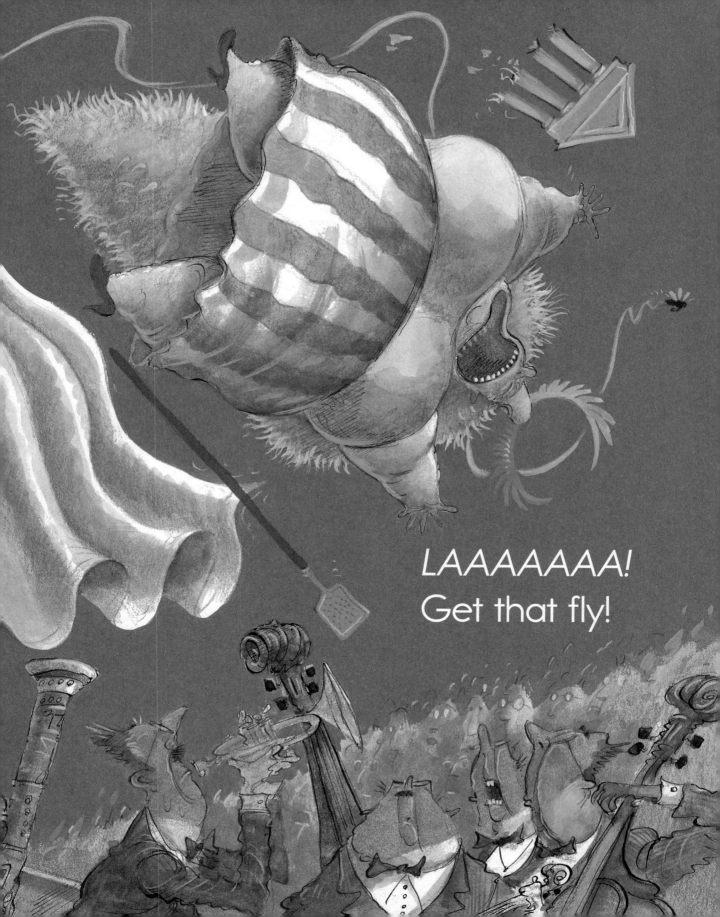

Oops!

The fly flew out.
Bye, fly!